Woodland Christmas

by

FRANCES TYRRELL

Woodland Christmas

by

FRANCES TYRRELL

North Winds Press
A Division of Scholastic Canada Ltd.

The illustrations for this book were done in
watercolour on Arches rag paper.

Typeset in Galliard
by IBEX Graphic Communications, Inc.

Canadian Cataloguing in Publication Data

Twelve days of Christmas (English folk song)
Woodland Christmas

ISBN 0-590-24430-2

1. Folk songs, English – England – Texts.
2. Christmas music. I. Tyrrell, Frances, 1959-.
II. Title.

PZ8.3.T8517 1995   j782.42162'21015248'0268
C95-930966-7

7 6 5 4 3 2 1   Printed in Canada   5 6 7 8/9

For our little cub, Neil.

The animals in this book are:
one gray partridge,
two rock doves, three ruffed grouse,
four common loons, five river otters,
six Canada geese, seven whistling swans, eight raccoons,
nine red foxes, ten moose, eleven red squirrels
and twelve beavers.
The bird in the potted pear tree
is a California partridge,
and the courting couple are black bears.

On the first day of Christmas,
My true love gave to me
A partridge in a pear tree.

On the second day of Christmas,
My true love gave to me:
Two turtledoves
And a partridge in a pear tree.

On the third day of Christmas,
My true love gave to me:
Three French hens
Two turtledoves
And a partridge in a pear tree.

On the fourth day of Christmas,
My true love gave to me:
Four calling birds
Three French hens
Two turtledoves
And a partridge in a pear tree.

On the fifth day of Christmas,
My true love gave to me:
Five golden rings
Four calling birds
Three French hens
Two turtledoves
And a partridge in a pear tree.

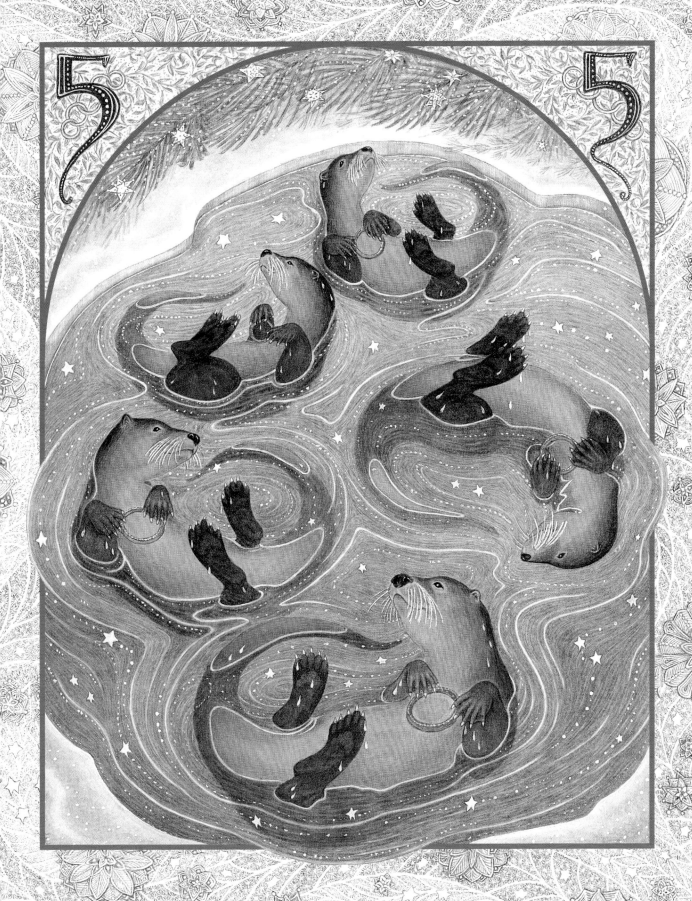

On the sixth day of Christmas,
My true love gave to me:
Six geese a-laying
Five golden rings
Four calling birds
Three French hens
Two turtledoves
And a partridge in a pear tree.

On the seventh day of Christmas,
My true love gave to me:
Seven swans a-swimming
Six geese a-laying
Five golden rings
Four calling birds
Three French hens
Two turtledoves
And a partridge in a pear tree.

On the eighth day of Christmas,
My true love gave to me:
Eight maids a-milking
Seven swans a-swimming
Six geese a-laying
Five golden rings
Four calling birds
Three French hens
Two turtledoves
And a partridge in a pear tree.

On the ninth day of Christmas,
My true love gave to me:
Nine ladies dancing
Eight maids a-milking
Seven swans a-swimming
Six geese a-laying
Five golden rings
Four calling birds
Three French hens
Two turtledoves
And a partridge in a pear tree.

On the tenth day of Christmas,
My true love gave to me:
Ten lords a-leaping
Nine ladies dancing
Eight maids a-milking
Seven swans a-swimming
Six geese a-laying
Five golden rings
Four calling birds
Three French hens
Two turtledoves
And a partridge in a pear tree.

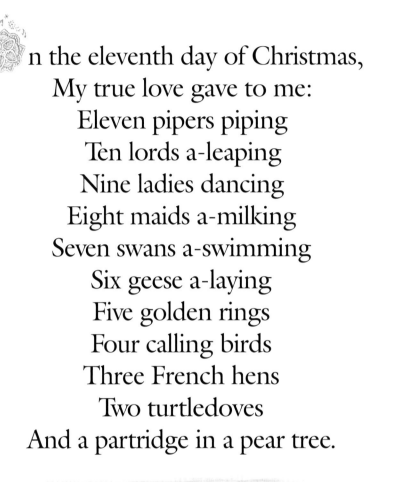

On the eleventh day of Christmas,
My true love gave to me:
Eleven pipers piping
Ten lords a-leaping
Nine ladies dancing
Eight maids a-milking
Seven swans a-swimming
Six geese a-laying
Five golden rings
Four calling birds
Three French hens
Two turtledoves
And a partridge in a pear tree.

On the twelfth day of Christmas,
My true love gave to me:
Twelve drummers drumming
Eleven pipers piping
Ten lords a-leaping
Nine ladies dancing
Eight maids a-milking
Seven swans a-swimming
Six geese a-laying
Five golden rings
Four calling birds
Three French hens
Two turtledoves
And a partridge in a pear tree.

The Twelve Days of Christmas